THE WIVES OF MACHISMO

PART 2

BY: SANDRA MORENO

The Wives of Machismo Part 2

Copyright @2020 Sandra Moreno

ISBN: 978-0-578-67966-2

Library of Congress Control Number: 2016909771

Sandra Moreno rev. date 05/14/2020

This book is dedicated to all the women of the world. May you love and respect yourself so much that you will never allow anyone to disrespect you. May you always have the motivation, determination, and strength to stand up for yourself. Never allow anyone to control, or abuse you. The moment you become fearful of a man, is the moment you should run and never look back. Be strong, be beautiful, be free, be you.

Contents

Living in Fear by the Train Tracks

Waiting in agony, in fear for her life, she cries as her body trembles

uncontrollably. The sound of the train signal is amplified in her head.

She watches the train signal arms go down. A vision of her mother appears

in her head, then another vision quickly appears, it was the moment when

she first met Juan Carlos. "Why, oh why did I smile back at him?" she asks

herself in desperation.

It was a rainy day and Yolanda got a flat tire on the highway. She turns on

her hazard lights and pulls over. She's never had a flat and doesn't know the

first thing about how to change a tire.

Everyone she knows is at work and she doesn't want to bother anyone.

She sits in her car listening to the rain coming down hard.

She's frightened by a loud sound of a knock.

She sees that it's a police officer. She rolls down her window.

"Ma'am, what seems to be the problem?" He asked.

"Ugh, I have a flat tire." She responds.

"Do you have a spare tire?" He asks while standing in the rain.

"Yes, I do, it's in the trunk," she said nervously.

"Pop your trunk open, I'll take care of it for you," he says.

"But, it's raining," she responds.

"It's fine, just open the trunk," he says, while walking towards the trunk.

She opens her trunk and watches him in the rearview mirror. Feeling so bad about the heavy rain and watching the police officer getting all wet, she grabs her umbrella and gets out of the car. She walks towards him.

"I'm sorry about this horrible rain," she says.

"It's fine, I don't mind at all." He says while noticing her bright red stilettos and her beautifully toned legs. Yolanda runs every morning to stay fit.

"Okay, all done." he says.

Yolanda hands him a twenty-dollar bill. "No, that won't be necessary," he says.

"Please take the money," she says.

"How about dinner? he asks, as he smiles at her.

She smiles back at him and they gaze into each other's eyes for a minute.

"Okay, she says with a smile, feeling like she's in a movie.

That was the beginning of a life she could have never imagined that she would be living.

She had no way of knowing that this handsome and kind man would put her through her worst nightmare.

Just a few months into the relationship, everything changed.

Juan Carlos would get drunk every day and come home accusing his wife of cheating on him.

When Yolanda first met Juan Carlos, she fell head over heels, and deeply in love with him.

Unfortunately, she spends her nights crying and constantly defending herself to Juan Carlos.

During these long, drunken nights, Juan Carlos bullies Yolanda in such a terrible way.

One night,

Yolanda was fast asleep at their cozy, two-bedroom, two bath home in the country, just a few miles from the city and Juan Carlos's job.

She's dreaming but she begins to hear the sound of the train. She starts to become uncomfortable. This is when her husband usually gets home; shortly after the midnight train.

The sounds of Juan Carlos stumbling and running into furniture wakes up Yolanda. She never knows if he wants to have drunken sex, or fight for hours. Either way, the sound of the train passing takes her mind off of what's going on.

Yolanda sits up in the bed and she sees Juan Carlos standing at the doorway of the bedroom.

"Was that my cousin's car that just left?" he asked, slurring his words and barely keeping his balance.

"What? No? I was sleeping." she responds.

"You're fucking lying to me!" He shouts.

"Go to sleep," she says softly to Juan Carlos.

"Look at you! You were fucking him, weren't you?" He yells.

"You're drunk, please, just go to sleep." begs Yolanda.

"No!" He yells again as he kicks the bed.

"Stop!" Yolanda cries out.

"Get up!" He shouts.

"No, I don't want to, I have to get up early and go to work." she says.

Juan Carlos pulls the covers off Yolanda. "Get up!" He yells again.

Juan Carlos behaved this way almost every night when he would get home from work.

He usually got tired and eventually would pass out, but tonight was different.

He grabbed her arm and jerked her off the bed.

He began kicking her repeatedly all over her body.

Yolanda is screaming in pain.

"Stop, stop, please stop." begs Yolanda.

He drags her out of the house and throws her in the car and jumps in right after. She tries to get out but he stops her.

Juan Carlos was in a rage.

Yolanda was terrified.

Feeling uncertain about what he will do next, Yolanda doesn't try to escape anymore.

Juan Carlos drives away like a mad man. He can barely stay on the road. He's driving at a high speed and swerving from left to right. Yolanda doesn't say a word.

As he begins to drive over the train tracks, he slows down.

He comes to a complete stop on the train tracks and puts the car in park.

He turns over to Yolanda.

"How long have you been fucking my cousin?" He asks.

"I'm not! Says Yolanda with tears rolling down her face.

"You better tell me how long you've been fucking my cousin or you will die right here on these train tracks," he yells.

"I already told you so many times, I'm not sleeping with anyone else but you, Juan Carlos." she says while crying out loud.

At that moment, Juan Carlos turns off the ignition and pulls out the keys. He throws them out of the car window into a grassy field.

"Oh my God!" She cries out while trying to get out of the car.

Him being much stronger than her, it doesn't take much for him to hold her down.

"Tell me! Tell me! How many times have you opened your legs for my cousin?" He yells with such hatred while slapping her over and over again.

She tries to put her hands over her face to protect herself.

"Please, let me out of the car! Juan Carlos, please?" Begs Yolanda.

He won't let her out of the car.

Suddenly, she hears the most terrifying sound of her life.

It's the train signal.

As Juan Carlos has her pinned down, she can see the red lights on the arms of the railroad crossing blinking. Her eyes get big and wide. Then, she sees the arms beginning to go down.

"Please, please, Juan Carlos, let me out." She pleads hysterically while squirming, trying to get loose.

Juan Carlos is so drunk and has no idea just how dangerous this situation really is.

She now hears the train horn.

She's panic stricken.

"Oh my God! No, no, please let me out." she continues to cry out.

"I've never been with anyone else but you! I promise! Please, please, you have to believe me," cries Yolanda.

The sound of the train is getting closer and closer.

Juan Carlos is still on top of Yolanda holding her down.

Realizing that she will never get loose in time, she stops fighting and closes her eyes.

The vision of her mother appears in her mind. She remembers that perfect day when her Mother was pushing her on the swing at the park. Her Mom's smile was so beautiful as she pushed Yolanda higher and higher. She remembers giggling and being so happy.

She knows that her life is coming to an end and she waits in agony for the train to hit the car.

Juan Carlos jumps up and grabs Yolanda. He opens the car door and throws her out. She rolls down this rocky hill.

Just as he's about to jump out himself, the train crashes into the car.

Yolanda lets out this horrific scream as she tries to get up off the ground. The train is going by so fast and is so loud.

It seems like forever that Yolanda stands there trembling and waiting for the train to be finished.

The train has finally passed.

She runs up the hill towards the tracks and looks around in a panic. There is no car, there is no Juan Carlos. Moments later, she hears an explosion. She can see a fire in the distance. She begins to hear the screeching sound of the brakes on the train. She starts to run along the tracks. She falls and gets back up repeatedly. Growing tired and out of breath. She can finally see the remains of the charred car at the end of the train. She stops and just stares.

She's in disbelief. Within minutes, the fire department arrives. The fire is put out. She watches a fireman look into the car and then hears him say, "we have a body."

Yolanda lets out a horrific cry and falls to her knees. She's trembling and crying in fear by the train tracks.

Going Out with The Guys

"I'm going out with the guys tonight," Says Fernando to his wife. "With who?" Replied Jessica.

"Just with the guys, don't get all paranoid. We're just gonna have a few drinks and hang out." he said.

Jessica feels unsure of this because during her ten-year marriage to Fernando, he cheats often and it usually starts when he goes out with the guys.

Jessica is always torn apart every time she finds out but she gets scared about leaving. She's very good at burying her feelings to avoid her having to deal with the situation.

She covers it up well, and portrays herself as a happy wife.

The family pictures are of a perfect family.

The worst affair for Jessica was when she was pregnant with their second child. She felt extremely insecure about her body. Especially because she was never able to lose all the weight from the first baby.

Fernando had gone out with the guys, and soon after, he became quite distant.

This happens often in their marriage.

A few weeks later, Jessica had found many pictures and text messages from one particular girl. She had the body of a pin up girl. She had a flat stomach with big breasts and a tight rear end. This girl also had long, blonde hair with big curls that outlined her pretty face perfectly.

The betrayal was evident in the text messages. They had swapped racy pictures back and forth while discussing all the times they had met, in great detail.

Jessica fell to pieces. Here she was eight months pregnant with swelling from head to toe, a big belly, and many stretch marks.

Jessica has always been petite with straight brown hair that she keeps at shoulder length.

Her petite body has changed over the years due to being pregnant and having a baby. Now, another one is on the way.

Jessica is dedicated to her family and it shows in all she does. She works part-time so she could have more time with her children as they are her world.

Fernando is spoiled by Jessica, who cooks delicious dinners and makes him hearty lunches every day.

Also, she keeps the house immaculate.

Fernando betrays Jessica over and over again, because he knows that she doesn't have it in her to do anything about it.

He's quite comfortable. He sleeps with any woman he chooses, and gets to come home to a clean house with dinner ready and his wife and kids at his side.

What a deal! He will never leave and neither will she.

The Stress Across Her Face

It's a hot and windy day in Texas, Eva is anxiously awaiting her lunch break.

Her husband, Carlos, of four years takes her to and from work and picks her up for lunch.

Carlos does not allow her to have any time away from him.

He does not have a job, nor a car.

He has never been able to keep a job and now that Eva is making a better salary, he relaxes at home and calls all the shots.

If Eva is late coming out for her lunch break, Carlos starts accusing her of sleeping around, with her co-workers. The arguments get pretty ugly and he becomes quite abusive.

It's twelve thirty and Eva stands up and grabs her purse. At that moment, her boss, Karen, walks up behind her.

"Eva, I'm sorry, you'll have to wait at least fifteen minutes before you can take your break. We're expecting guests. You can go to lunch after they've visited your area." said Karen.

Eva instantly panics. She already knows that her husband will be so upset that she's not outside at her normal break time.

"Karen, may I go to the restroom, please?" asks Eva in a nervous tone.

"Of course, honey, go right ahead," says Karen.

As Eva is walking towards the restroom, she looks back to make sure nobody is looking, then she quickly makes her way into one of the offices with a phone.

She calls Carlos numerous times, but no answer. She goes back to her work area in a hurry.

The people that she works with can't help but stare at her, because they can see that she's so uneasy all the time.

The stress across her face is seen by all.

Eva is now free to take her lunch break.

She's extremely nervous and shaking, knowing that her husband will be very upset.

She sees Carlos sitting in the car waiting for her. She gets in the car.

"Hi, baby, I'm sorry that I..."

She feels a hard slap across her face.

"Babe, I couldn't help it."

Again, another slap across her face.

Eva cries out loud.

"No, Babe, please, stop." she sobs.

"Who are you sleeping with now?" yells Carlos.

"Nobody, I promise." cries Eva.

"I'm sitting in the car like an idiot and you're inside screwing another man!" yells Carlos.

"No, I'm not. My boss wouldn't let me leave at my normal time." Eva explained.

"You're making me suffer, so now I will make you suffer," he said, "You will not be eating lunch today."

"Babe, I need to eat something, please? I haven't eaten since yesterday." pleads Eva.

"No, you will not eat." says Carlos as he pulls the car into a grassy area and parks the car. He turns off the engine and just stares out the window.

It's almost a hundred degrees out.

"What are we doing? Where are we?" asked Eva.

"Don't worry about it." says Carlos.

"It's so hot babe, I can't sit in this hot car." she says as she opens the car door.

Carlos reaches over her and shuts the door then locks it.

"No, you're not going anywhere," he says.

"Oh my God!" she cries.

"Please let me open the door, Carlos." she begs.

"I already told you that you're going to suffer just like me. So, shut the hell up or I'll slap you again." Carlos shouted.

Eva is dripping sweat and the car is so hot that she can barely breath.

Finally, Carlos starts the car again.

Eva was so relieved as she felt the cold air from the air condition blowing on her face.

She wasn't hungry anymore.

Carlos takes her back to work, then he heads home to take a nap.

Keeping her head down, Eva walks into the ladies restroom and quickly splashes cold water on her face. She then dries off her face and the rest of her body.

She's embarrassed because her shirt is soaking in sweat. .

As she heads back to her department, everyone just stares at her as they always do.

Eva is only twenty-eight years old, but because of this exhausting lifestyle, she's aging fast.

This goes on every single day.

Everyone can see the stress across her face.

She Doesn't Love Him Anymore

Lisa just finished bathing the children and has put them to bed.

Gabriel, her husband of fifteen years is a man who has always provided a nice life for his wife and kids.

Lisa always waits for Gabriel at the door so she can watch him pull up into the driveway.

Although Gabriel is a cold and distant man, Lisa is very much in love with him.

Every morning as Gabriel eats his breakfast that Lisa has made, she also prepares lunch for her hard-working husband.

She places little love notes in his lunch box hoping to reach her husband's farfetched heart.

Gabriel never says anything about the notes.

Ever since Lisa met her husband all those years ago, she's made her whole life about Gabriel.

Lisa keeps herself quite busy working as a stay at home Mom. She takes wonderful care of her family and her home.

She doesn't have any friends but that's her choice.

Growing up, Lisa's Dad hardly ever spoke to Lisa's Mom. This was normal in the Mexican culture.

Men didn't have conversations with their wives. They were the breadwinners and the baby makers.

Years go by and Lisa is growing tired of catering to her husbands every need.

Gabriel doesn't find notes in his lunch kit anymore.

Soon, he feels a great distance between the two of them.

Gabriel notices that Lisa doesn't wait for him at the door anymore.

Eventually, she doesn't even get out of bed in time to make her husband breakfast or lunch either.

Lisa is now quiet and distant with Gabriel.

One day Gabriel walks up to Lisa and asks what's wrong with her.

She replied, "I don't love you anymore."

She Resists

She can feel his body against hers. Her heart is beating loud and hard in her chest. She's been so lonely for too long.

Irene has worked in the marketing department for a large corporation for thirteen years.

She's been married to Javier for twelve of them. They do not have any children. It just never happened.

When Irene met Javier, he spoiled her with flowers, perfume, fancy dinners and jewelry.

This all stopped the day they got married.

Irene first noticed Javier's sudden rudeness at their wedding. She thought that maybe she misread his mood. It was a full and busy day with so many people that she didn't pay a whole lot of attention to it.

From that day forward, everything had changed.

Irene is so in love with Javier and he was ignoring her completely.

She had no idea what had happened.

They made so many plans and Javier had made so many promises to her, only to leave her feeling so empty.

She attempted talking to him almost every night. He would brush her off. He would say that he's tired.

"How can a relationship go from hot to cold so fast?" Irene often wondered.

"Javier, can we go out to dinner tonight?" asked Irene one Friday evening.

"I'm not hungry." replied Javier.

"We don't talk, we hardly ever make love, what's wrong?" asked Irene.

"I'm just tired, okay?" responded Javier.

"No, it's not okay." said Irene.

Javier walks out of the room.

Irene is devastated but often continues her attempts to get close to her husband.

She doesn't lose hope that one day her husband will look at her and find her attractive once again.

Luckily, her job keeps her very busy so she doesn't usually dwell on this for very long.

When the company hires a new assistant and he's assigned to help Irene, she's instantly attracted to him.

There's something about this man that has her adrenaline soaring every time he walks in the room.

After several weeks, the feeling is so intense.

Irene finds herself thinking about this man all the time.

When she sleeps, she dreams of him.

While driving, he's on her mind.

One morning as Irene is looking out her high-rise office window, she doesn't hear her assistant walk in.

Suddenly, she feels his body from behind. He presses up against her.

She gasps for air; she smells his hypnotizing cologne.

"I locked the door." he gently whispers in her ear while moving her long hair away from her neck.

She doesn't move. She can feel her body getting warm all over. She can feel an amazing tingling beginning at her feet, and slowly traveling upward. Her legs begin to go numb, then she feels a hypnotizing sensation between her legs.

She would love nothing else but to turn around and let him ravish her.

"I can't do this." she says.

"I want you so bad." he says softly.

"Please stop. I can't do this." says Irene in a nervous, crackly voice.

"Why are you resisting me? He asked.

"I'm married." she replied.

"Please, don't resist me any longer." he says.

"I must." responded Irene.

Later that day, still in a trance she goes home.

She walks in the door and sees Javier on the couch watching television.

"I'm home." she says.

Javier doesn't respond.

She walks closer to him.

"I'm home." she says in a louder voice.

"I heard you the first time." he rudely replied.

"Well, you didn't say anything." says Irene in a sad tone.

There's no response. Javier keeps watching tv, not being phased by his wife's presence.

She walks into her bedroom to change into something more comfortable.

Irene spends the entire evening thinking about her assistant.

She skips dinner and prepares a nice, hot bubble bath for her.

Irene steps into the tub and submerges her silhouette body into the warm and bubbly water.

All she can think about is how her assistant made her feel. She hasn't felt those sensations running through her body in a very long time.

Weeks go by and the attraction between her and her assistant is almost more than she can handle.

Javier continues to be cold and distant to her, while her assistant continues brushing his body against hers every chance he gets.

She resists.

She's Too Comfortable to Leave

It's a long drive home on these Texas highways for Marissa. She had to leave suddenly the week before to go see her father who became very ill and was hospitalized.

Once her father was out of the woods, she headed back home.

Marissa and her husband Charlie of three years, have a two-year-old son.

Marissa is twenty-two years old, with a slim body and ivory skin. She has full lips, medium length golden brown hair with pretty highlights, and she always has her fingers and toes done beautifully.

Marissa married Charlie right out of high school and has never worked.

Charlie has always provided a nice life for her and her son.

She pulls up in the driveway around midnight, relieved to be home, she lets out a sigh of relief.

She's only been gone for seven days but it seemed like an eternity for Marissa.

She walks in slowly trying not to wake anyone up. Her husband, her aunt Maria and her son are sleeping.

As Marissa is getting ready for bed, she hears Charlie's cell phone constantly vibrating.

Charlie is fast asleep and doesn't hear a thing.

Marissa picks up the cell phone and sees several text messages coming through.

She frowns as she reads the name of the person who is sending these messages.

It says, Candy.

She looks over at Charlie who doesn't realize that she is home and looks back at the phone.

She begins looking at all the messages that this so-called Candy has sent her husband.

It's picture after picture of seductive photos and long messages about a steamy two-day stay at some hotel.

Marissa is shocked and deeply saddened.

She cries and cries all night long.

The next day, she confronts her husband about what she saw on his phone.

"It's just someone I met; we didn't do anything." says Charlie.

"The messages say something different." says Marissa as tears roll down her face.

"She doesn't mean anything to me." Charlie says.

"Where did you meet her?" asked Marissa.

"At the sports bar down the road." replied Charlie.

"That tacky club, with all those raunchy, half dressed, trashy girls?" asked Marissa.

"You shouldn't talk about those girls like that" says Charlie.

"You're taking up for them?" asked Marissa.

"At least they work," says Charlie in a rude tone.

"Well, then, I'm going out, too. says Marissa.

"You're not going anywhere!" shouts Charlie.

"Why can't I go out?" she asked.

"That's just how it is!" he yells.

"That's not fair at all." Marissa replies in disbelief.

"It's a guy thing, that's all. Calm down, nothing happened." says Charlie as he left for work.

Marissa knows what she read on those messages. She knows for a fact that her husband was unfaithful.

She feels that she's not able to leave him because she doesn't work. How would she support herself? She didn't want to raise her son without his father. She also doesn't want to leave her son at daycare while she works. She enjoys staying home with their two-year-old son.

Marissa is young and beautiful but doesn't have the courage to leave her husband, so she decides to stay in her comfort zone and do nothing. Although, she knows that her life will be filled with numerous affairs and betrayal, she's too comfortable to leave.

Wandering Eye

As Bianca is flipping through each piece of clothing in the clearance section of a department store, her eyes shift to her husband, Chris.

She sighs in disappointment as she can clearly see his eyes staring down a woman across from him.

Chris makes it a point to wear sunglasses everywhere he goes, especially where he knows that there will be women. He thinks nobody will see his wandering eye.

Little does he know; his wife sees everything.

Many Mexican men have a disrespectful habit of staring at women, not looking, staring, making women feel very uncomfortable. These women can almost feel these men stripping them down with their eyes.

This type of behavior is not only uncomfortable for the women being stared at, it's extremely disturbing for the wives of these men.

These men enjoy going everywhere with their wives, to the doctor, the mall, the children's school or the grocery store. They're not there to support their wives, they do this to feast their eyes.

"Can you stop?" Bianca whispers under her breath.

"What?" asks Chris.

"You know." responds Bianca.

"I don't know what you're talking about." replies Chris.

"I can see your eyes." says Bianca.

"Here we go." says Chris.

"I can't cover my eyes. I can't help it if there are beautiful women everywhere." he says.

"Beautiful? Wow. You never tell me I'm beautiful." replied Bianca.

Chris grunts and lets out a deep sigh as he walks off.

Bianca is saddened.

Although Bianca tries to bite her tongue and not say anything, sometimes it's hard not to.

Instead of reassuring Bianca, Chris always gets mad and storms off in a huff.

Later that week, they both attend a family barbecue.

Bianca makes her special chocolate brownies with pecans. She drizzles fudge syrup on top right before she puts them out. Everybody flocks to Bianca's brownies with excitement.

The family raves over these brownies as they dig in.

It's a fun Saturday afternoon. They're all in the backyard laughing, talking and listening to music.

Suddenly, Chris's cousin, Hector arrives with his new girlfriend.

Chris immediately pushes his sunglasses up high on his face to hide his eyes as he begins to stare slowly up and down at this young girl.

Chris gets up and walks over to her.

"Where have you been all my life?" he says to this girl.

"Chris, this is Jessica." says Hector as he laughs and shakes his head at his cousin's remark.

Feeling leery about this older man, Jessica is instantly uncomfortable. She tries her best not to frown. She doesn't want to come across as rude, after all,

It's her first-time meeting Hector's family.

Bianca is just a few feet away and sees all this take place.

Once again, she's saddened.

"I used to have a body like that." thinks Bianca to herself as she looks at this girl wearing tight blue jean shorts and a white tank top with only flip flops on her feet. Her long black hair blows in the wind. You can't help but notice her perfect skin tone, like a porcelain doll.

Bianca just turned fifty years old and has been married to Chris for almost thirty years.

They have four children that are now grown and have moved out on their own.

Although Bianca has a thicker body than most women that she's around, she carries herself well, always dressing very nice and smiling everywhere she goes.

Her big heart and willingness to always help others attracts many to her.

Bianca feels happy and confident everywhere she goes, except when she's with Chris, that's when her confidence goes out the window.

Chris has always had a wandering eye and Bianca carries a knot in the pit of her stomach because of this.

She knows that she can't compete with young girls which seems to be her husband's favorite eye candy.

Chris always looks for just the right spot to sit at. Always with the perfect view.

He's able to watch this young girl's every move behind those sunglasses.

Bianca feels her heart beating fast as she is very upset.

Not wanting to spoil a family barbecue, Bianca bites her tongue and doesn't say a word.

Knowing that this is the lifestyle that she will always lead with her husband, she sighs.

One day, the phone rings. It's their son, Michael.

"Hi, Mom, just letting you know that I'm stopping by later this afternoon with some friends to shoot some hoops. Is that okay, Mom?" Michael asks.

"Of course, it is. I'll prepare some snacks." Bianca replies.

"Thank you, Mom, you're the best." says Michael as he hangs up.

Bianca and Chris are sitting at the table finishing their quiet dinner when they hear Michael coming through the front door with his friends.

The house feels alive with all the commotion.

"Hi, Mom, Dad, we're here and we're starving." says Michael as he hugs his Mom tightly.

"Hi guys, there's plenty to eat, so dig in." says Bianca as she smiles.

"Wait, I don't know you? "asks Bianca as she looks over at a new face.

"Hi, I'm Tony. How are you? "says this young man as he puts his hand out.

Bianca shakes his hand and smiles as she can't help but to glance up and down and this ribbed young man wearing a muscle shirt and gym shorts. He has short, black hair and striking blue eyes. Bianca is caught off guard by this surprising feeling of an attraction to this young man.

In a trance she continues to shake his hand.

She slowly stops and let's go.

Feeling a bit jealous, Chris frowns at his wife's loopy behavior. Bianca watches as the boys eat. She keeps looking at Tony. Her eyes lock into his lips as he takes every bite. She's being visually seduced by this attractive young man.

"Thanks, everything was delicious, the boys say as they head to the backyard where the basketball goal is.

"You're welcome." Replied Bianca.

Chris is still bothered as he looks on.

He gets up and walks over to Bianca.

"What the hell was that?" He asks.

"What?" She responds.

"You? The way you were looking at that kid." He says in an upset tone.

34

"Really? You're going to tell me something about looking at another guy? The one that looks at every girl. everywhere we go? replies Bianca in a sassy tone.

Chris is pissed and storms out of the room

Bianca fills the sink with hot, soapy water and begins to look out her kitchen window.

Now, she's the one with the perfect view.

She grabs the sponge and very slowly begins to wash her dishes.

It was as though she was massaging her dishes as she was staring at the sweaty body of this young man.

Tight abs, sculpted arms, a firm bottom and tons of energy is what Bianca was mesmerized by.

Bianca was breathing heavily and began to feel warm all over, something she hadn't felt in years.

Her husband walks back into the kitchen.

The way Bianca is washing the dishes, stops him.

"Like what you see?" He says, in a deep voice.

"Oh, ugh," she says as she gets tongue twisted and fumbles with the dishes almost breaking them.

"What the hell, Bianca?" Chris shouts.

"I can see clearly what you're thinking." He says,

"Oh really, what am I thinking, Chris?" She asks.

"You want to sleep with him so bad, I can see it. The way you're just staring at him. My God, look at you. You're acting like a hot whore wanting to get laid." He continues shouting.

"How dare you talk to me like that?" She says,

"You're disgusting!" He shouts.

"All those years of you staring at every woman you see, wearing those dumbass sunglasses as if I can't see what you're looking at? How do you think I felt all those times? I felt like you were acting like a horny bastard, that's how I felt, but I never said those words to you. "She yells back.

"Men just look at women, there's nothing you can do about that." Responds Chris.

"So, it's okay if you act like a horny teenage boy around all those girls?" She asks.

"Yes, it's just how men are." Chris responds.

"Well, guess what? This is the twentieth century and it's about time that women catch up to their sneaky husbands and start doing some of the same shit they do. If you don't like it, that's just too bad." Bianca says in an angry tone.

"Oh, so you're going to start doing this from now on?" Asked Chris.

"Yes, if you can stare at women as you always do, then it's about freaking time that I start looking at men. Get one thing straight though, I won't be wearing sunglasses." Bianca responds in a smart-ass tone.

"You don't think that I'll put up with this type of behavior from my wife, do you?" Yells Chris.

Bianca is angry thinking of all those times that he didn't think twice about her feelings when he was staring at all those other women.

"Okay, well then you need to stop looking at other women, too." She says,

"No, that's never going to happen. It's natural for men to have a wandering eye." Chris responds in a firm tone.

"Okay then, to even things out, from now on, I will have a wandering eye, too, and there's nothing that you can do about that either. Now, I'm going to take a cold shower right now," she says as she leaves the kitchen.

With tight lips and anger in his eyes, Chris glares at Bianca walk away.

Although Chris is not happy with his wife's new behavior, Bianca feels exhilarated.

Now they both have a wandering eye.

This House Is Cold, Quiet and Still

It's a cold winter morning and snow is falling like rain. The house is cold, quiet and still.

Rebecca gets out of bed and slips on her baby blue robe and matching slippers.

She walks slowly through the house feeling great emptiness in her heart and soul.

Not wanting to wake her husband, she tiptoes her way to the kitchen.

She prepares her coffee as quietly as she can.

Rebecca is seventy-two years old and has been married to Gabriel since she was sixteen.

He began abusing her shortly after they started dating.

She married him anyways.

They proceeded to have four children who are all married and live elsewhere with families of their own.

Rebecca has lived her whole married life under the control of her husband.

She was never able to work or have a life outside the home because Gabriel would not allow it.

She obeyed.

Although they live a calm and quiet life as they are both in their seventies, the abuse has never stopped.

As Rebecca is enjoying her cup of hot coffee, she hears a noise.

Her heart falls into the pit of her stomach.

He's awake.

She takes a deep swallow and can feel her heart begin to race.

She hears his footsteps coming towards her.

She sits quietly on the couch and waits for it.

Rebecca then tenses up and clenches her teeth.

At that moment, she feels what feels like a bolt of lightning shooting through her body.

Gabriel has punched Rebecca with a closed fist on her head.

This is something he does every day as he walks by his wife of fifty-six years.

She has new and old knots on her head. She has to be so careful when she brushes her hair.

As her green eyes fill with tears, she takes another deep swallow.

Rebecca feels great sadness about the long life of abuse that she's endured

Her husband and family is all she knows.

Not having any friends or anyone to talk to, she never knew what to do about this horrible abuse.

If she would have only left Gabriel the first day, he laid a hand on her, her life would have been completely different.

Instead, she stayed. Only to live a long life of heartache.

The house is cold, quiet and still.

Her First Crush

Danielle wakes up to the sound of heavy rain hitting the roof of their home in the beautiful hills of California. Their house is one of many nestled among thousands of trees.

She slowly opens her eyes. Her body is feeling as stiff as a brick. Running up and down those bleachers at school for P.E. have caused some aching muscles for sure.

Not wanting to move, she stays in bed listening to the rain.

Suddenly, her phone vibrates loudly on the nightstand next to her bed.

She leaps out of bed with great energy knowing exactly who's texting her at six o'clock in the morning.

It's a message from him. Him, being the one guy that caught her eye when she started her freshman year in high school.

Danielle was never interested in having a boyfriend until she met him.

His name is Jacob.

All the girls in school are crazy about him.

He appears to be shy. A young man of few words. Something about his silent demeanor attracts Danielle to him. He has dark brown eyes and short dark hair, with a clean-shaven face. His skin is light and his lips are full. He has a thin build with defined arm muscles. The fact that he's a senior in high school doesn't matter to Danielle.

The school year is almost over now. Summer is just a few short weeks away.

It was only last week that Danielle had given her phone number to Jacob.

He began texting her immediately,

Danielle reaches for her phone to view her message.

"Good Morning Beautiful." is what Jacob has texted.

Danielle smiles and just as she's about to text back she hears something break. It was coming from downstairs.

"Danielle!" Shouts her mother.

"Help me, Danielle, quick, please hurry," screams her mother.

Danielle tosses her phone on the bed and runs downstairs.

Her mother is on a step stool and has dropped a handful of plates on the tile floor in the kitchen. There is broken glass everywhere.

"Mom, oh my gosh, don't move. Let me get this cleaned up." says Danielle in a panic as she reaches for the broom and dust pan.

After several minutes, the glass is finally off the floor and her mother can come down from the stool.

"Thank you, sweet girl." says Danielle's Mom to her.

Danielle races upstairs to get back to texting Jacob.

As she approaches her phone, she sees that Jacob is now calling her.

"Hello." She says softly.

"Where were you?" said a gruff voice on the other end.

Danielle knows it's Jacob on the phone.

"I had to help my Mom." Said Danielle.

"Sure, you did." Responds Jacob rudely, as he hangs up the phone.

Danielle is shocked and confused. She calls him back several times but he won't pick up.

Although upset, she gets ready for school. She knows she'll see him there.

On her way to second period, Danielle stops at the water fountain to get a drink when she suddenly feels someone grabbing her arm in a harmful manner.

She looks up right away.

It's him.

"Jacob, you're hurting me, "says Danielle as her eyes are beginning to fill up with tears.

"You better respond to my text messages and answer my calls quickly. You hear me?" He says in an angry tone as he squeezes her arm tightly.

Many look on and witness this behavior but nobody says anything. They just walk away and whisper among each other.

As Danielle is leaving school, her friend, Savannah rushes to her.

"Danielle, I saw what Jacob did to you today. Danielle, you shouldn't let him treat you that way," begged Savannah.

"That was my fault." Replied Danielle.

"No, it wasn't your fault," said Savannah.

"You don't know him." Responds Danielle.

"Neither do you," said Savannah.

"He loves me." Says Danielle with tears rolling down her face.

"That's not love!" Shouts Savannah not being able to control her volume because she's so upset and worried about her friend.

"Shh, keep your voice down. Don't make a big deal about it." Says Danielle as she looks around to see if anyone heard.

"When a man hurts a woman, it most certainly is a big deal. It's wrong." Says Savannah with great concern in her voice.

Danielle walks off.

As Danielle gets home, she begins to fumble through her backpack for her house key when Jacob jumps out of the bushes.

She's startled.

With his big hand, he grabs her throat pushing her against the brick.

"I thought you had soccer practice? Yells Jacob.

"It was cancelled." Replied Danielle.

"You're lying to me!" Shouted Jacob.

"No, I'm not lying." Cries Danielle.

Jacob runs off.

Later that night as Danielle is getting out of the shower, she hears her mom's voice.

"Honey, I'm home. Want to go out for Chinese? Dad is going to meet us there." Shouts her mom from downstairs.

"Oh, I don't know. I'm kind of tired." Replies Danielle.

"What? You're passing up Chinese? Who are you and where is my daughter?" Asks Danielle's mom in a silly tone.

"All I want to do is go to bed." Replied Danielle.

"Well, okay then. I'm heading out. Love, you." Yells her mom.

"Love you, too, mom." Responds Danielle.

Shortly after her Mom drives away, Danielle climbs into her bed and begins to doze off.

The doorbell rings.

Her eyes open and she wonders who could be at the door.

The doorbell rings again.

She gets up and wraps her robe around her slim body. Her hair is still wet and not brushed but she goes towards the door anyways.

As she peeks through the peephole, she sees that it's Jacob.

She disarms the alarm and opens the door.

He pushes the door in with force.

"Wait, I'm not dressed, "says Danielle.

"Was someone here with you?" Says Jacob in an upset tone.

"No, nobody was here." She replies.

"You're lying to me." Yells Jacob, as he pushes her down to the floor with full force.

" I would never lie to you," Shouts out Danielle as she tries to get back up.

Jacob pushes her down again.

"Stop, Jacob, you have to believe me." Cries Danielle.

"You know what? Don't call me," Jacob says as he makes his way towards the door.

"Jacob, please don't leave, I love you!" Shouts Danielle as she's filled with uncontrollable emotion.

Jacob stops and turns around.

"You mean that?" He asks.

"Yes, Jacob, I love you." Danielle says with tears rolling down her face.

He walks towards her. He wipes her tears from her face. He then kisses her.

"I love you, too, that's why I get so crazy around you. I love you so much and you're my girl and nobody else's. You hear me?" He says as he holds her chin with a firm hold.

"Yes, I hear you. You don't have to worry. Jacob, you're the only one for me." Cries Danielle.

"Good." says Jacob in a macho tone as he turns around and walks out the door.

The relationship between Danielle and Jacob becomes extremely intense over the summer.

Danielle is so in love with Jacob and has allowed him to take full control of her heart, mind, body & soul.

She's blinded by her first crush.

Lies & Betrayal

Helen pulls up in her driveway on this warm afternoon. She notices the trash cans still in the street, and the overgrown weeds in the flowerbeds. Her husband's truck is in the driveway yet again. Her husband Eddie has been coming home early for many weeks now, and he's always in the restroom. This time, she walks in quietly. She puts her ear to the bathroom door to listen. She hears his voice.

"Oh yes! Show me more! Yes! Keep showing it to me! Yes! Don't stop! Oh, yes! Yes! Yes! Keep showing it to me! Yeah Baby! That's it! Ahh!!!" yells David as he reaches his exploding pleasure. Helen covers her mouth in disbelief.

Then, at that moment, Helen hears a young girls laughter, echoing.

"Will you show it to me again tomorrow?" Eddie asks, as he's trying to catch his breath.

Only if you beg me for it, says the girl on the phone, as she continues to giggle.

Helen quickly pulls the door open.

Eddie drops the phone on the floor as he panics.

Helen looks down and sees the face of a young girl on Eddie's phone.

Eddie grabs the phone with his dirty hands and ends the video call immediately.

His secretions are all over him.

"What the hell is going on?" Asks Helen.

" Nothing, baby." Replied Eddie.

"What do you mean nothing?" Says Helen in an emotional tone.

"You're cheating on me?" Helen questions.

"No, I'm not cheating." Replied Eddie.

"Then, what do you call this?" Asked Helen in a shaky voice.

Eddie shuts the door and locks it. He gets cleaned up before coming out.

"You just had sex with someone else!" Shouts Helen.

"No, I didn't." says Eddie, as he puts his pants back on.

"Yes, you did." Cries Helen.

"I'm alone in this bathroom." Says Eddie in a smart-ass tone.

"No, you most certainly were not alone." Yells Helen with tear filled eyes.

"After twenty years of marriage and three kids, I can't believe you're doing this." Cries Helen.

"Doing what?" Asked Eddie as he opens the door.

"Cheating, that's what you're doing!" Shouts Helen.

"No, no it's not. That girl wasn't even here. I don't know her personally." Replied Eddie.

"Eddie, it's the same thing. Having sex on a video call or in person is the same. You're having sex with another woman." Says Helen.

"Men do this all the time. It's not cheating." Shouts Eddie.

"I want a divorce!" Screams Helen.

"A divorce? What are you talking about? No, Babe, you don't know what you're saying." Says Eddie in a more sincere tone.

"You had sex with another woman and that's grounds for divorce! We're done!" Yells Helen as she starts packing her bags.

"Stop." Says Eddie as he tries to put Helen's clothes back in the drawers.

"Don't touch my stuff, you disgusting pig! Helen screams.

"You can't leave, come on, you're my wife, I love you. Stop doing this." Eddie says in a sad tone as he realizes Helen is really going to leave him.

"No, Eddie. You don't love me. You're having sex with other girls over your phone. I'm filing for divorce tomorrow." She says while zipping up her suitcase.

"Divorce?" You're crazy! On what grounds?" He questions.

"Cheating! She says, while crying.

"The girl was on the phone. That's not grounds for a divorce." He responds.

"Cheating is cheating. In person, online, on the phone. It's all cheating. You have betrayed me in such a horrible way. I'm heartbroken." She shouts.

"I refuse to be another one of those women who stay with a man who has to relieve himself sexually to other women." She says while crying hysterically.

Eddie is in disbelief as he watches his wife leave him.

Heartbroken

The skies are blue and the sun is beginning to set on this September day.

There's excitement in the hallways of this prestigious office building as the clock hits five.

"Have a good weekend," is all you hear from many people as they're feeling joyful that the work week has finally ended.

Valentina is joyful as well as she grabs her purse and tote bag. She heads out the door.

Everyone is smiling and heading to their cars talking about their weekend plans.

Valentina smiles at them as she gets into her car.

She lets out a sigh of relief as she starts her engine.

She turns on the radio, and tunes in to some smooth jazz music, which is her favorite weekend music.

Although she's stuck in traffic, she's carefree and humming to the music.

Valentina is thirty-four years old. She stands about five foot and ten inches tall; her skin is light and she has a curvaceous body with a bubble bottom that pops no matter what she wears. She has big brown eyes, and wears a smile everywhere she goes.

She's been married for sixteen years to Marco.

She met him when she was seventeen years old. This is while she was on the rebound from her first boyfriend, which was possessive and abusive.

Marco had come to her rescue and promised her that he would take care of her and treat her like a queen.

He was passionate about spoiling her and keeping her happy, at the beginning anyways.

Once they had their children, daughters now seven and five years old, Marco became distant and macho. He became a man of few words

There was no more hugging and holding each other for them.

The only thing that kept this home alive was the laughter of their little girls.

Marco was on auto-pilot. He would go to work, come home, play on the floor with the girls for a little while, eat dinner, watch tv, take a shower and go

to bed.

He hardly ever spoke to Valentina.

Every morning Valentina wakes up to the sounds of her husband getting ready for work.

She often sits up in bed and tries to talk to Marco. He hardly ever responds.

Just as he is about to leave for work, he walks towards Valentina and plants a hard, emotionless kiss on her lips. Valentina is left with such an empty feeling all the way down to the pit of her stomach.

Marco lives his life doing what he wants, when he wants, never including Valentina in any of his plans.

Finally, Valentina is home. She pulls up in the driveway and slowly gets out of the car. She's trying to hang on to the happy thoughts about it being

Friday.

"Mommy, mommy!" shout the girls as they run to the front door hearing that their Mom just walked in.

Valentina kneels on the floor and embraces her children.

Valentina looks around for Marco. She spots him sitting on the couch just a few feet from her.

Marco is six feet, two inches tall. He has olive toned skin, and green eyes with a slender build.

Valentina finds her husband incredibly handsome, even to this day.

Still hugging the girls, she looks at Marco waiting for him to turn his head and acknowledge that she has walked in the door. He never does.

Marco obviously knows that Valentina is home from work but he continues to watch tv and flip channels on the remote control.

Valentina will sit down next to Marco when she sees him watching television just to be near him but Marco will automatically get up and hand her

the remote and goes to watch tv elsewhere.

Valentina often feels a cold chill run through her body. She feels a heavy feeling in the pit of her stomach, it's called heartache.

Marco's actions speak loud and clear; her existence doesn't matter to him.

Friday is just another day in this household. There are rarely any plans made.

This is depressing for Valentina. She's always hoping and wishing that her and Marco will do something, anything.

Most of the people that they know go out to dinner and maybe have drinks to unwind and socialize on the weekends.

There have been rare occasions that the two of them went out to dinner. Unfortunately, when it's just the two of them, Valentina feels like she's

dining with a stranger. Sadly, even when they have dinner at home, there is rarely conversation. Valentina tries hard to make small talk but Marco just keeps on eating without even looking at her.

If Marco has plans, they are usually for him only. Valentina will not know he has plans until she sees that Marco is getting dressed to go somewhere.

"Where are you going?" She'll ask.

"Somewhere," He responds in his macho tone.

There are some Sunday mornings that Marco will tell Valentina that he's going to the grocery store while he's getting ready to go. Not caring that it's

a last-minute thing, she quickly gets dressed just to spend time with Marco. Although, they don't talk much, Valentina is happy in her heart just to

spend time with Marco even if it is just tagging along for a trip to the grocery store.

Valentina puts a lot of effort in keeping herself happy for the sake of the girls. She doesn't want them to feel her sadness.

All these years of Marco's distant behavior and Valentina can't get used to it. Some days, she grins and bears it, while others, she sobs. She's Heartbroken.

His Guilt is Covered by Gifts

Martin takes his wife, Alicia on a four-day trip to Napa Valley. He's arranged for the kids to be kept by his Mother. Alicia awakes to the sound of Martin's whispering voice. "Good morning, beautiful," he says softly.

She stretches her well rested body and yawns. She opens her eyes and sees her husband. "Good morning," Alicia says as she smiles.

Lately, Martin has been feeling insecure due to his guilt. He knows he must constantly do things to keep his wife happy so that she always thinks that everything is okay between them.

Alicia received a call recently from a strange woman letting her know of her husband's extra marital affairs.

Alicia doesn't believe it and feels that the woman is lying because in her mind, there's nothing wrong with her marriage.

She confronts Martin anyways. Of course, he denies it completely, but he's left feeling very guilty because it's true.

Martin is having a couple of affairs. This has been going on for several years.

There is Lyndsey, the girl that gives him everything he could ever want in the bedroom. She's single and is always ready and available for Martin anytime he gets the sinful urge. She for-fills his every naughty need. Sadly, for Lyndsey, she's very much in love with Martin. The fact that he's married doesn't matter to her empty soul. Their sexual encounters fill the void in her life, for a while anyway.

And then there's Letty. The one. The one his heart truly skips a beat for. The one he would leave his wife for in a heartbeat. He loves this girl so much but she's married. Although, they both deeply love each other, and have such strong chemistry, they will never be together as a couple because Letty will never leave her husband and she's made that very clear to Martin. They don't see each other as often as they used to because their love for each other is so strong and this brings much heartache to the both of them. Martin loves his wife as well but this is more of an obligation. He has kids with her and doesn't want another man to have her or his children, so he often comes up with new ideas on keeping his wife happy. A last-minute trip and exquisite gifts is his ticket to staying married to Alicia. She will never know that she's not the love of her husband's life.

His Guilt is Covered by Gifts.

Strip Club

It's almost 2am on this foggy morning. The city lights can barely be seen in this busy part of town. Inside this small club, the music is loud and the dancers are hot. At a small table in the back, all you see is blond hair whipping around. This erotic dancer is wearing nothing but a white string thong bikini. It's clear to see that she's enjoying her work. She giggles as she pulls off a business tie from one of her favorite customers. She then wraps the tie around her neck and shakes her large breasts in front of this gentleman's face. Every now and then, she lets her hard nipples brush across his face, ever so gently, she knows that this drives him crazy. The more she excites this man, the greater the tip. His name is Esteban, a Spanish man in his early thirties. He has a dark complexion and stands about five foot, nine inches tall. He has a muscular build. This is due to his loyalty to the gym. He's hard core in his work outs and all who sees him can't help but notice. His white button up shirt has been loosened enough so the dancer can slide her hands in and caress his chest every so often. Esteban sits there with a handful of money, and Carly, his favorite dancer of all, is working hard for her tip money. Although she's barely old enough to work there, she knows exactly what turns a man on. At the very end of every dance, there's a little icing on the cake for Esteban, as she bends over to touch her toes with that hot ass in Esteban's face, using her finger, she slightly moves her string bikini over a bit so he can get a close-up view of her furry little slit. Esteban explodes in his pants every time she does this.

He then drops all his money for her.

Soon, the club is closing. He gets up and hits the men's room to clean himself up before he leaves. "Wait," says Carly as she sees Esteban heading towards the door. He turns around and she runs to him and kisses him ever so passionately. His body tingles all over.

She's working him well to be sure he keeps coming back.

He's left short of breath and completely infatuated with Carly.

As he gets into his car, he smiles in disbelief at how this girl makes him feel. He turns on the ignition. At that point, he remembers that he has a wife and new baby at home

Esteban has a dreadful drive home.

He finally arrives and makes his way to the bedroom. As he walks in, he stumbles because he's quite intoxicated. He slams his foot into the crib, which is in their room right now. The baby starts crying. Isabella wakes up. They have a two-month-old son and he's the spitting image of his father. You would think Esteban would be elated and enjoying his new son. On the contrary, he doesn't want to be home. All he can think about is his special dancer at the club. "Where have you been?" Asked Isabella.

"Out." Responds Esteban while kicking off his boots.

"You're hardly ever home." Says Isabella with a frown on her face. "What's the point in being home? You're always with the baby anyways." Shouts Esteban. "Our baby." Cried Isabella. Esteban gets into bed and within minutes, he's sleeping. He's not adapting very well to being a father. He's even lost interest in being a husband. Isabella gets into bed. She lays there with her eyes wide open. She's not sleepy and many things are running through her mind, like all the weight she gained during her pregnancy, her husband's rudeness towards her and why he never wants to be home.

She hopes that Esteban will see past her imperfect body and make love to her soon. She's initiated it several times but he always pushes her away. She's yearning to be held, to be loved, to be kissed, and especially to be made love to. Isabella is definitely having the blues, but not the baby blues, it's marriage blues. A whole week goes by and although Esteban has been coming straight home from work, he hasn't been speaking to Isabella at all. This is driving her crazy. She's severely depressed at this point. She thinks that Esteban is feeling overwhelmed with the new baby and maybe doesn't know how to handle his Daddy role. The last thing that she would suspect is another woman. It's a warm and muggy evening in Texas and Esteban has had enough of the homelife and is heading to the club. He's so excited about seeing his favorite girl. He stops at a local flower shop to buy a dozen red roses, and he has the florist add some ribbon and baby's breath. He wants to impress Carly. Driving to the club, he begins to sing to the song on the radio. Esteban is feeling so alive. He doesn't ever remember feeling this way about anyone. He's high on life with such incredible excitement running through his body, like a kid having his first crush. Carly is on his mind twenty-four, seven. As he walks into the club, she spots him and smiles at him from across the room. With a hand signal, she calls him to a back table. "You brought me flowers?" She asked as she puts them up to her nose to smell them. "Thank you." She says with a sweet voice. This petite young girl holds all the power when it comes to Esteban. He's head over heels for her. He sits and gets comfortable. Carly begins her erotic dancing for him. Meanwhile, back home, Isabella is rocking lil Esteban to sleep. She sings so sweetly to him. Those precious brown eyes looking into hers make her heart melt. It's amazing to her how much she loves her baby. It saddens her that Esteban doesn't feel the same.

Tonight, Carly has a romantic evening planned to get her husband's attention. She even put the crib in the nursery tonight. Once the baby was asleep, she quietly walked him to his crib. She grabs the baby monitor and then walks over to her bathroom and begins by taking a shower. She slips on a pink lacy nightgown. It's loose fitting but it hangs on her body nicely. She pulls up her long wavy brown hair into a clip. With not much time to spare, she puts on a small amount of eyeliner, lip gloss, and a small spritz of perfume on her neck. She goes to lay on the bed to wait for her handsome prince to come through that door and ravish her. She positions herself in a sexy pose. She waits. . . She falls asleep.

Hours go by and Isabella is awakened by the sound of the shower turning on. She fixes herself up a bit and continues to lay there. She closes her eyes pretending to be asleep waiting for Esteban to see her when he gets into bed. Next thing you know, he climbs into bed and turns his back to Isabella. She quickly opens her eyes and is staring at Esteban's back. She places her hand on his shoulder. He pushes it off. "Esteban, what's wrong?" Asks Isabella. "I'm tired," He replies. "Esteban, look at me?" She begs. He doesn't move or say anything. She touches his shoulder again. "Look at me, she cried. "No," He says without looking. "What's wrong," She asks as she sits up in the bed. "Please look at me," Esteban. Finally, he turns his head over to look at her. "What are you wearing? What are you doing?" He asks in disgust. "Esteban, I put some makeup on for you tonight." She says, "Why?" He asks as he turns his back to her again. "Esteban, I thought we could make love tonight." She says, as her voice shakes because she feels like he is going to reject her. "What? No, that's not happening." He says in a rude tone. "Why not?" Asks Isabella. "Just go to sleep," Esteban replied. "Sleep? No, I don't want to go to sleep. Come on, baby." Isabella says, as she touches Esteban's back. "I said no!" says Esteban in a gruff voice. He has no desire to be with his wife. All he can think about is Carly. Tears roll down Isabella's face. She's so hurt and saddened at Esteban's behavior in the last several months. He's not only an absent dad but he's an absent husband, too. She lay there listening to Esteban snore for hours before she finally fell asleep. The next morning as she's feeding Lil Esteban in his room, she hears Esteban leaving for work. He never looked for her or Lil Esteban. No goodbye kiss for neither one of them. Her heart falls into the pit of her stomach as she hears him drive away. The next several weeks are exactly the same. There are nights that Esteban doesn't get home until two in the morning. Then, there are some nights that he gets home early and will go look in on Lil Esteban for a few minutes before he takes a shower and goes to bed. He never wants to eat dinner at home anymore. Isabella has been throwing out his dinner almost every night because he's always refusing to eat. It was a Saturday morning and Esteban was just getting out of bed. He was reminiscing about the night before. Carly was incredible at the club and he couldn't get her out of his mind. Isabella walks into the bedroom and sees Esteban stretching. She puts both of her hands on his chest. "Stop! Yells Esteban as he pushes her hands off of him. "What in the world is wrong with you, Esteban!" Shouts Isabella. "I just…" mumbles Esteban. "You, just what?" Questions Isabella. Esteban is quiet. He doesn't know what to say but he knows that he doesn't want to be around her anymore. The love he once had for Isabella is completely gone. He's aware that he has a new baby but Carly has stolen Esteban's heart leaving no room for anyone else in it. "Esteban? Are you seeing someone else?" asked Isabella with tears rolling down her face.

"Yes," He replies. The darkest feeling enters Isabella's body. She stands there in shock. "How could you do this to me? To us? Esteban, we have a baby. How could you do this? Are you in love with this woman? Say something." She cries. Esteban takes a deep breath. "Yes, I am." he finally replied. "You are what?" questioned Isabella. "In love with her." Replied Esteban. "What about me? What about us?" Isabella asks as she sobs. "Did you have sex with her?" shouts Isabella. "Not exactly." He replies. "What does that mean?" She questions. "It's hard to explain, she's, well, she's." "What the hell, Esteban? She's what? Spit it out!" Yells Isabella. "She dances for me." He responds. "Dances for you? Is she a stripper? or what?" She replies. 'Yes, she is." says Esteban. "All these nights? You've been going to a strip club? And, now you're in love with a stripper?" She yells. "You don't understand." He responds. "What's there to understand? That you're in love with a stripper? No, I don't understand that!" She shouts. "I'm so disgusted with you!" Get out! I can't even stand to look at you. Go move in with your stripper!" Shouts Isabella. Esteban goes into the bedroom. He stands there and just looks around. He's not sure what to do. Then he realizes that this is his ticket out of the marriage. He will be free to be with Carly. He goes into the closet and reaches for his duffle bag that he has on the top shelf. He unzips it and starts grabbing bunches of clothes off the hangers and stuffs the bag. He makes his way to the bathroom to grab his shaving kit and toothbrush. Although he's leaving his wife, he's excited because all he can think about is being with Carly. He can finally make love to her, ravish her, live his life with her, and show her off to his friends. As he walks out of the bedroom, he sees Isabella in the hallway holding Esteban Jr. Tears are rolling down her face. Esteban turns away and walks out the door. Sadly, the fact that he's leaving his baby doesn't affect him at all, after all, he's been infatuated with Carly since before the baby was born. As Esteban is driving to the club to go see Carly, his mind is racing. Feeling like his life has just begun, he begins making many plans in his head for his future with Carly. He finally arrives at the club. Feeling a burst of energy, he quickly turns off his car and walks inside the club. He's earlier than usual. He looks around but doesn't see Carly. "Is Carly here?" Esteban asks one of the waitresses. "She's in the back," replied the girl. He walks to the dressing room. He knocks lightly. "Come in," Says a faint voice. He pushes the squeaky door open. Esteban pokes his head in the door. Carly is looking in the mirror while putting on her mascara and sees Esteban in the mirror. She's startled by Esteban's presence. "What are you doing back here?" Asked Carly. "I came to see you,' Replied Esteban. "You're not supposed to come back here. You need to go back out there. I'll be out there soon, `she replied. "But I have some news." He says, she walks towards the door and signals for him to go out. "Wait, I needed to tell you that I left my wife today. I'm a free man. Carly, we can now be together." Says Esteban with so much emotion. "What? No! We can't be together. Why would you think that we can be together?" She replies. "Carly, I love you. You're all I ever think about." Says Esteban, as he puts his hands on her face. She grabs his hands and gently pushes them away. "Oh no, you've mistaken my work for something else," She replies. "I know you love me, too," Replied Esteban. "No, I don't love you. This is my job, it's what I do for a living. Please get out of the dressing room." She says in a disappointed tone. Wait, wait, you do love me, I can tell by the way you dance for me and all the other things that you do to me," Replied Esteban. "I do this for all of my clients, Esteban. This is my work." She replied "But, I love you." He replied. "No, no, you don't love me, you just think you do." Carly replied with great disappointment in her voice. "Please, give me a chance. I can be the man you want and need in your life." Replied Esteban. "Listen, to me. I've never wanted a man in my life. I'm completely happy with my partner in life. She's a woman, and I'm madly in love with her." She replied. "A woman? No, no way. Why did you trick me into making me believe that you love me? The way you dance for me, and the other things that you do to make sure that I'm completely satisfied. How could you have done this to me? Says Esteban with tears in his eyes. "Like I said, it's my job. This is what I do to make a living. I'm sorry but I can't dance for you anymore. Please leave and don't ever come back." She replied.

Stunned, Esteban walks out of the club and gets into his car. He drives for many hours, then, finally makes his way to his best-friend's apartment. Esteban only has one friend and his name is Jacob. He confesses everything to his friend. "You're such an idiot!" Replied Jacob. "You have what every man dreams of having; a knock-out of a wife who loves you, and a new baby boy who looks just like you. That's all shot to hell for a stripper? You've got to be kidding me?" Says Jacob while shaking his head. "I messed up, I guess. I let myself fall in love with somebody that wasn't real." Says Esteban, as he puts both of his hands over his head. "What are you going to do now?" Asked Jacob. "Leaving town for a few months. I'm going to stay with my brother. I need to clear my head. Maybe, when I return, Isabella will be ready to take me back.

Several months later, Esteban returns. He walks up to the front door of his home. As he gets closer to the door, he hears laughter in the house. He thinks twice about using his key since he's been gone for so long. He rings the doorbell. Esteban hears the laughter getting closer to the door. The door opens. It's Jacob and Isabella at the door, still laughing, until they realize who's at the door. "Esteban?" Says Jacob. Esteban is shocked to see Jacob at his home. "What are you doing here? Asked Esteban. "I live here." Replied Jacob. Esteban looks over at Isabella. "It's true, Esteban. Jacob's been incredible, with me and baby Esteban. He loves us both and says that he can't live without us. We've already been to see a lawyer to have divorce papers drawn up. You'll get half of everything." Says Jacob. "Do you want to see Esteban Jr.?" Asked Isabella. Esteban feels dazed and confused. "No, no, I don't." He responds. Esteban turns around and walks back to his car. He sits there for a long time. He breaks down and cries. He stares at his home and realizes that he had it all, and he blew it. His family is broken because he went to a strip club.

The Perfect Widow

Jill sits across the table from Jesse as they discuss business. She stares into space, as she listens to the rain hitting the window. Jill has been forced into running her late husband's business. He died suddenly just a month ago. It was heartbreaking. Jill had been out shopping on a Sunday afternoon, and came home to find her husband dead on the kitchen floor. She thought that he'd had a heart attack but the medical examiners autopsy report showed that he had choked on his sandwich. She had only been married for seven years and has inherited a company that she has no clue on how to run. She calls Jesse, one of the employees. She asks him if he would come over and go over the business with her. Although Jesse knows how strikingly attractive, she is, and he knows it may become an issue for him, he agrees. All of the guys at the company refer to her as Barbie. Jill is exactly that. She has blonde hair, large breasts, that she paid good money for, a small waist and a full bottom. Jill comes from money and has had many cosmetic procedures to make herself absolutely perfect in every way. People can't help but stare at such perfect beauty. Although she's in her fifties, the work she's had done makes her look much younger. She's also never had children, so, she's managed to escape the major changes a woman's body goes through during pregnancy. Jesse has been with the company the longest and definitely has more knowledge than the others. They schedule a day for the following week. Jesse just had his sixtieth birthday and has been married for almost thirty-nine years to Sabrina, his high school sweetheart. They have four children and several grandchildren. Unfortunately, Jesse has never been faithful to his wife. His affairs had usually been brief. The other women in his life have often been the girls in the offices that he's worked in. He's an electrician. To Jesse's advantage, he gets to meet several young women on a daily basis. These girls know he's married but that just intrigues them more. Sabrina only knows of two affairs. This was in the beginning of their marriage. Jesse was in his twenties at the time. Little does she know, he's never stopped having affairs, not for long, anyways. She has suspected this from time to time because Jesse hasn't touched her romantically in over ten years. Sabrina has tried to discuss this with Jesse, but he says that he's just tired and always cuts the conversation short. She finds it hard to believe that his reason for not wanting to have sex with her is that he's tired, but she accepts it. It's a cool Thursday morning and the rain is heavy in the city of Providence when Jesse arrives at Jill's home. They immediately jump in and start talking about the key factors of the business they do, he notices that Jill has tuned out. "Jill? Jill? Jesse says. She continues looking out the window which overlooks the well-manicured lawn. Jesse, who is sitting right across from her, reaches across and taps her shoulder. "Oh, sorry" she says as she turns to look at Jesse. "Are you okay?" asked Jesse. Tears roll down her face. "I'm so lost without him." Says Jill as she puts her head down and covers her face. Jesse stands up and goes around the table. He puts his hands on her shoulders. "I'm really sorry. I miss him, too." says Jesse in a low voice. Jill stands up and puts her arms around Jesse. She hugs him real tight, as she sobs. Even in this sad moment, Jesse is quite excited about this beauty in his arms. He can feel her breasts against his chest. She slowly puts her arms down and holds his hands. She looks into Jesse's eyes. "Please take care of me." She asks. "Of course," replies Jesse. She holds onto his hands a little longer than she should, and he's completely aware of this. They both know exactly what's going on. "See you next Thursday," she says. Jesse nods his head. "I'll be here, bright and early," he says, as he raises his eyebrows. Jesse never gives it much thought at the fact that he has a wife. He doesn't see Sabrina as a sexy woman. In Jesse's eyes, there is no comparison between his wife and Jill? Remember, she had a lot of beautiful work done to her. Sabrina is a beauty herself, but she's all natural. Although she's shapely, there is some extra weight on her, she doesn't have anything perfect on her body. There has never been enough money to alter any part of her body, nor has she ever given it much thought. She's tall with a medium build and has long black hair. Her eyes are big and brown and she has a smile that can light up any man's heart, except her husbands. Sabrina works out a few times a week to stay healthy, but she's not obsessive about looking perfect. It's been several years now since Jesse cares to have sex. Sabrina often wonders if this is healthy for their marriage. She has confronted Jesse many times about this but he always says that he just doesn't think about sex anymore. Jill has been very unhappy about this because this has often been the only form of communication in their marriage. This leaves her feeling quite lonely. She would never have thought that her sex life would be over while she was in her forties, but it is. She's never been okay with this, but she has simply accepted the fact that she will no longer be intimate with a man for as long as she lives.

Jesse continues going over to Jill's home on Thursday's. Each time he goes over, Jill wears less and less clothing. She's luring him in, slowly. Jesse is so turned on and can't think of anything else but his perfect Barbie. He often relieves himself in the shower just thinking about her. His mind is completely consumed by Jill. Sabrina feels quite lonely but keeps herself busy with work, caring for her children, and her aging parents. She doesn't dare discuss this with anyone. She's so ashamed that her husband doesn't want her anymore.

It's five o'clock in the morning and Sabrina is awakened by the sound of the shower. She frowns knowing that Jesse took a shower the night before. "Why did you take another shower?" Asked Sabrina as Jesse steps out of the bathroom. "I just wanted to take a shower, is that okay?" he replies in a rude tone. Not to make things worse, Sabrina drops it. Jesse leaves shortly after. Jesse is feeling this great rush throughout his body. He's so horny just thinking about Jill's hot body. He can't wait to see what she will be wearing today. The thought of those large breasts and that long blond hair makes him so hard. He looks down at the bulge in his pants, as he stops at a red light. Jill is his new interest, and this won't stop until he sleeps with her. He rings the bell. "It's open." He hears from afar. He goes in. He looks around but doesn't see her. He walks through her living room and into the study which is where they conduct business. He's a bit nervous and sits down. He finally hears movement. "Hey." She says softly, as she slowly grazes her hand across his shoulders. That touch makes Jesse's head spin. Jill sits across from him.

"Shall we get started?" Asked Jesse, as he let out a big sigh. Jill looks at Jesse and just stares at him for a few seconds. He instantly feels the attraction. "Why don't we do this in the bedroom?" she says, with smile. She's been working on him every chance she gets, and today may be the day, the day that he plunges into her with all his might. She can hardly stand the wait anymore. She wants a man inside of her so bad. He stands up and walks around the table. He grabbed her by her tiny waist and lifted her up, throwing her over his shoulder. They're both laughing with excitement. He finally makes it through her bedroom door. As he threw her on the bed, he moans loud and falls to his knees at the foot of the bed. Jesse moans louder and louder. Jill wraps her legs around his neck. She's so wet and so hot. She's waiting for him to rip off her lacy panties and lick her snatch until she explodes in sinful lust.

Then, nothing is happening. There is no movement. There is silence.

Jill sits up on the bed. She sees Jesse on the floor "I can't move!" He yells, as he lays on the floor in excruciating pain. "What can I do?" She asks. "Call 911", he responds. He's taken to the hospital where he was later admitted. He is forced to call his wife.

"In the hospital?" Sabrina repeats to Jesse on the phone. "Yes," he says in shame. "What happened?" She asked. "I lifted some heavy material," he replied. After many tests in the hospital, Jesse was diagnosed with several herniated discs, a hernia and a pulled groin. Needless to say, he won't be having sex anytime soon. While Jesse is in the hospital, Jill replaces Jesse with Javier, a much younger man. He's quite the handyman. There's nothing that he can't lift. Jill is quite happy with his strength and stamina, and Javier is completely satisfied with his new job.

Sabrina had a strong feeling that her husband got injured during sex. It was just a gut feeling. This was something that she just couldn't shake off. When she was in her twenties, she was able to brush off her husband's affairs, but now being in her fifties, she couldn't. She realized that her husband wasn't too tired to have sex, he just didn't want to have sex with her.

  This was enough for her to divorce Jesse.

Now that she's divorced, she's found herself thinking of all the men she's turned down because she was married. She is now single and can't wait to start exploring intimacy again. She decides to give in to the lawn man. He's been flirting with her for many years. He's in his early thirties, and that's perfect for Sabrina.

She has to make up for a lot of lost time,

and wants someone who can perform for hours.

This all happened because of the perfect widow.

Yearning to be Held

Gina unlocks her front door and walks in. All you hear is the sound of her high heels on the wood floors. She drops her keys into the glass bowl that sits on the buffet table next to the kitchen. Off to the bedroom closet she goes. She kicks off her heels, and takes off her business suit. She changes into a pair of black yoga pants and a gray t-shirt. She looks in the mirror as she whips up her long, brown, wavy hair, and secures it with a clip. She walks down the hall, heading towards the kitchen. As she approaches the study, she sees her husband sitting at the desk. She stops at the door. "Hi." She says to him, knowing she'll get little or no response. "Hey." He mumbles, never looking away from the computer. "I'm going to cook dinner." She says, "I'm not hungry." He responds. Gina has been married to Nick for almost twenty-five years. They're both in their late forties. Gina hasn't adjusted to Nick not paying attention to her anymore. He's been distant for quite some time now. The communication and intimacy in their relationship has come to a complete halt. She never thought her sex life would be over this early in life. She's tried to talk to Nick about this on several occasions but he always gets angry and walks away. As the years go by, Gina loses her confidence and self-esteem. She's truly saddened and often feels like less than a woman.

Although difficult, she's trying to adapt to Nick's cold demeanor towards her. Years later, while at work, someone new has transferred to her department. His name is Diego. Talk about tall, dark & oh so handsome. It's hard not to notice how incredibly attractive he is. Gina has found herself staring at him numerous times. She can't help it. She's knows she's just looking, after all, he's like twenty years younger than her. She begins training Diego on a new machine at work. They are together at work every day. One day as they're working, Diego notices that Gina has been crying. "You okay?" He asks. "I'm fine" She says harshly. "No, you're not. Is it your husband making you sad? He questioned. "This is nothing new, I'll be okay." She replies. "Gina, please know that I truly care about you. It's been quite difficult to respect the fact that you're married." Diego says. Gina turns and looks over at him in disbelief. "I'm so much older than you." She says in shock. "Gina, your age doesn't matter to me. The truth is that I've fallen in love with you. You're incredibly sexy and I want you so bad." Diego says with passion in his eyes. Someone walks into the office and Gina walks out quickly. She sure doesn't want anyone seeing them alone together. She already feels guilty. As the weeks go by, Diego consumes Gina's thoughts. No matter what she's doing or where she's at, she's always thinking of Diego. She begins to feel warm sensations run through her body just thinking about him. She never thought that she would ever feel this way again. It was getting quite difficult to work with Diego. Every time he walks in, she melts. As she was closing up the office one day, Diego walked in. She turns to him and says, "the office is closed now. Everyone has left. Did you need something?" She asked in a shaky voice, knowing that something may happen right about now. "Yes, I need something alright, and I'm looking at her," he responds. She felt excited and scared at the same time. As he came near her, she could feel the warmth of his body. Suddenly, her heart was pounding harder and harder. She began to breathe heavily. She felt as if she was going to faint. When he brought his lips close to hers, her body tingles all over. When their lips finally touched, she felt magical. The incredible feeling throughout her whole body made her feel so weak, and so wonderful at the same time. She was slipping into another world. It was heavenly. He grabbed her by her hips and pulled her close. Their bodies were touching as he caressed her lips with his tongue. She could barely catch her breath. She felt that she would climax at any moment. "Escape with me?" He whispers in her ear. The feeling of his warm breath and lips touching her ear make her go into a trance. He begins kissing her. They're tongues are tangled in passion. It seems like a lifetime ago that she was kissed like that.

He takes off her blouse and begins kissing her neck. This sends beautiful goose bumps throughout Gina's body. He slowly wraps his arms around her and removes her bra.

Her breasts are now free. Free to receive all the passion that she's been missing. Diego starts licking and sucking her nipples. It's been so long since she's felt this incredible passion. She's loving every erotic sensation. His lips and tongue start traveling down. "Oh my, oh, he's going down." She's thinking to herself while squirming and going crazy. Diego spreads her legs apart, and slowly puts his head between her legs, kissing and licking her inner thighs. Then, finally, oh yes, she feels the most incredible feeling as his tongue touches her clit. He begins licking, and licking her over and over, taking his sweet time, as if he's enjoying a delicious ice cream cone.

Hardly breathing, Gina climaxes many times. He unzips his pants, allowing his large and hardened penis to escape. He plunges into her wet garden. She lets out a yell and moves her hips along with him as he pushes and pumps into her over and over. She's panting in bliss and he's enjoying every second if it. He yells as he climaxes. Gina lays completely still on the big chair that they've now made a mess of. She's in disbelief. She cannot believe she's just had the most incredible sex of her life. She thought she would never experience this ever again. "I love you. Move in with me?" He whispers in her ear. "I wish I could." She responds. "You can, all you have to do is pack your things and come over. I'll be waiting for you.' He says.

As Gina begins to put her clothes back on, she's thinking about what Diego has asked her.

Later that evening when she gets home, the usual happens, her husband is not fazed by her presence. He keeps watching television and flipping channels, even though he hears that his wife is home from work. Gina goes into the bedroom and packs her bags. She passes back though the living room as she takes some of her belongings out to her car. Her husband never looked her way. She drives away. Gina knows that this thing with Diego may or may not last, but she's going to have the time of her life while it lasts. She files for divorce the next day.

Ignorance is Bliss

Sylvia awakens after a long night of tears. She slowly pulls the covers off of her. All you hear in is the sound of slippers hitting the tile floor. Lack of sleep has left Sylvia exhausted. She puts coffee on, then grabs her cell phone as she heads to the kitchen table. She sits and begins looking through her phone. Her husband never came home last night.

She checks to see if she has any missed calls from him. This is not the first time he's done this. The last time he did this, he was gone for three days. Sylvia had even filed a missing person's report with the local police department. He returned home alright. It had been evident that he had many days of alcohol and women. His neck and chest were covered in these small red marks. These marks are known as hickeys, or some would say, passion marks. Sylvia remembers the feeling of shock and sickness when this had occurred. Her husband, David had tried to convince her that these were pipe burns that he had obtained at work. Although she didn't believe him, she accepted it and never addressed the issue any further. It hasn't even been a year since that happened. She puts her phone down and walks over to the coffee pot where she pours her a cup. She walks over to the window facing the driveway and just stares, and listens to his car, but all she hears are the birds chirping on this sunny Spring morning. Sylvia walks over to her phone and checks the time. She's scheduled to be at work in less than an hour. She calls her boss and lets her know that she won't be in. Sylvia is a clerk at the Nueces County Attorney's Office in Corpus Christi, Texas. Although she loves her job, she knows that she won't be able to go in to work. Not only is she sleep deprived, but she doesn't have any inclination of David's whereabouts. She will not be able to work under those circumstances. Sylvia has several cups of coffee but still remains dazed. The sound of the noon bell coming from the church across the street startles her. She realizes that the morning has slipped by, and there's still no sign of David. Tired of sitting and sobbing, she decides to take a shower. All she can think about is the unknown. Not knowing if David is lying dead in a ditch somewhere, or, if he's with another woman. She's in agony. She dries off and wraps her long black hair in a towel. She reaches for her robe on the back of the door that she hadn't closed all the way. It slowly swings open, and that's when Sylvia notices Daniel laying across the bed, fully clothed and fast asleep. "David! Where were you?" Sylvia questions with, what she's not sure is the feeling of relief or anger. David pulls the pillow from under his head to over his head without saying a word. Using both hands, she pulls the pillow off of his head. He jumps out of bed and grabs her by the throat with both hands and has her against the wall and begins to choke her. "You don't ever question me, you hear me." He yells. Sylvia is filled with fear, as tears roll down her face. She smells the alcohol on his breath and doesn't say a word. David let's her go and goes back to bed. Her body slides down to the floor where she cries for hours. Later that day, she cooks dinner for the both of them, and once again, she doesn't deal with what has just happened. The next day as Sylvia is doing laundry. She notices lipstick on David's shirt. As she looks closer, she can smell women's perfume on it as well. Now, she knows for a fact that her husband was with another woman the night he didn't come home. Even though she's not surprised, she's still heartbroken with this confirmation. She knows that there's no need to confront David about this. He will deny it and become angry and abusive. She would rather not deal with it, so she does nothing. Months turn into years and Sylvia remains married to David. She lives her life knowing that her husband is unfaithful. She has never been a wife who snoops, or look through her husband's wallet or phone. Why look for something that she knows she more than likely won't deal with. She would rather sweep any abuse and infidelities under the rug and pretend it never happened. Sylvia does very well to ignore it all. Although she's abused and betrayed, she'd just rather not rock the boat. She continues to post happy pictures of the two of them on social media. Ignorance is Bliss.

My Husband Doesn't Like Me

"Lety! Lety! Get your ass in here!" Yells Marcelo as he stands in the kitchen filled with family and friends. There was a birthday party going on and they were all ready to sing happy birthday to the two-year-old little princess. "Marcelo, you shouldn't talk to your wife like that." Says his mother. "Well, she shouldn't be outside." Says Marcello. Lety runs in the house. "Finally," Says Marcello in a harsh tone. Family and friends have often witnessed Marcello being rude to his wife for most of their fifteen-year marriage. "I was walking some of our guests out," explains Lety in a soft voice. Lety has always been meek and has never talked back to her husband. She always bows down to Marcello. The end of the party has arrived and the last person has left. Lety walks into the kitchen and sighs as she looks at the trail of dishes. She begins the torturous cleanup. Marcello sits on the couch the whole time looking at his phone. The only voice you hear now that everyone has left, is Chloe's, as she talks to her dolls. Thanks to Marcello, there is little to no communication in this marriage. Lety feels lonesome on a daily basis. Almost an hour went by and the dishes were finally washed and put away. "I'm going to give Chloe a bath," says Lety as she walks through the living room. Marcello doesn't say a word. His eyes never move from his phone. Filling the tub with warm water, Lety gets lost in her thoughts. Minutes later you hear Chloe. "Mommy! Mommy! the water is spilling everywhere!" Lety jerks, as she is startled. "Oh no, I'm so sorry

sweetie," says Lety," as she throws some towels down on the floor, and

releases some of the water out of the tub. "Can we sing, Mommy?" asked

Chloe. "Of course, sweetie," responds Lety with a smile. "Merrily, merrily,

merrily, life is but a dream." sing Chloe and her Mommy, while giggling.

"Keep it down!" yells, Marcello, from the living room. Chloe's eyes get big.

She then puts her finger over her mouth. "Shh, Mommy. We can't sing

anymore. Daddy doesn't like it." whispers Chloe with pouty lips. Lety stares

into Chloe's eyes and is heartbroken for her. Marcelo has a way of making

his family feel bad for having fun. After Lety puts Chloe to bed, she walks

slowly throughout the house turning off lamps, and making sure the doors

are locked. She stares out the front window looking at the lamp post that

lights up the lawn. A strong feeling of loneliness comes over her. Lety enters

the bedroom and hears Marcello snoring. She scurries over to the closet and

grabs her gown and goes into the bathroom. She turns on the water and

prepares for a quick, but steamy shower. Exhausted, she finally climbs into

bed. Just as Lety is falling asleep, Marcelo rolls over and begins caressing

her legs. She knows all too well what that means. Lety is so tired, but she

wouldn't dare reject Marcelo, that would ignite the fire to his anger. Marcelo

starts kissing Lety's neck. She is sickened by the touch of his lips on her

body. He then gets on top of her. He uses his knees to open up her legs. Lety

wants to vomit. She can't stand this horrific feeling of being violated. She is so close to throw him off of her. Marcelo feels like a complete stranger to Lety, and she absolutely cannot stand him. She grins and bears it, but it's getting harder for her to deal with this. The next day, Marcelo is getting home from work as Lety is in the kitchen preparing dinner. "What's that awful smell?" he asked as he laid a harsh kiss on Lety's cheek. "I'm cooking dinner," she responds in a shaky voice. Marcelo can never say anything nice to his wife. Lety never feels good about anything that she does because Marcelo insults her constantly. With each passing day, the emotional pain and loneliness become almost unbearable. The following day, she takes Chloe to the doctor. While checking in, she realizes she doesn't have her insurance card. Suddenly, she gets anxious knowing she has to call Marcelo for the identification number. Marcelo rarely answers her calls, and if he does, he's rude. It's just the way it's always been. Lety tries her best to never call him because of this. Marcelo can ruin Lety's day in an instant. David's harsh words cut her like a knife. The fact that Marcelo can make Lety cry in an instant, makes him feel macho and in control. She calls many times. Marcelo never answers. "Ma'am, if I don't get that information from you in the next five minutes, you will not be able to keep this appointment, and you will be charged the no-show fee." says the lady behind the desk. "Please, it will just be a few minutes, I just have to keep calling, my husband will answer my call eventually.

"she says in a panic. "Your husband?" asks a deep voice at the far corner of the waiting room. Lety's head turns to see whose voice that was. "Over here." says a man as he lifts his hand and waves. "Oh, yes, my husband." she says nervously. The other people in the waiting room look at this man and then back at Lety. "Excuse me for saying this, but you're radiant, your little girl is precious, and you're saying that your husband doesn't answer your calls? Sounds to me like your husband doesn't have a clue how lucky he is." says the man in a southern accent, as he tips his hat. Lety couldn't help but notice how attractive this man is. It's been a long time since she's ever been attracted to a man. "Thank you, that's very kind of you to say." replied Lety in a surprised manner.

She watched him as he spoke to the lady behind the desk. "Ma'am, I'll go ahead and take care of that fee you're adding on to this young lady's account. The lady smirks while looking back at him. He pulls out his wallet and lays a fifty on the counter. "If there's any change, kindly give it to this young lady. "Mr. Lawson, you can come on back," says a nurse, holding the door open. "If you want to be loved by a real man, call me. I'll take care of you. I promise the good Lord that." Says the man to Lety, as he hands her over his card. The touch of his hand sent goosebumps throughout her body. She felt warm all over. Although she had to reschedule Chloe's appointment, she didn't care. She was enjoying feeling this way. She never thought she could feel that way again. She then realized just how awful her husband treats her. It took a complete stranger to make her feel like a princess.

Suddenly, she felt her worth. When she got home, she packed her and

Chloe's bags. They were gone by the time Marcelo got home from work. He

looks all over for Lety. He sees a note on the table. He picks it up. It reads,

"To whom it may concern: For so many years, my husband didn't like me,

but yet, he expected me to love him. At this point in my life, I cannot stand

the sight of him. I must go and experience what it's like to be loved. Yours

Truly, Lety"

" Marcelo's eyes grow bigger, his heart begins to race, he then crumbles the

paper and throws it across the room.

Behind the Makeup

Waking up on Sunday morning is usually relaxing for most people. This is never the case for Flora Delgado. She lives with her husband, Edward of ten years, in the town of Midland, where the Summer consists of record-breaking temperatures. This Texas heat is no joke. Flora lay there in bed. She begins to hear the sounds of the ceiling fan. It wobbles pretty bad and one of the blades is missing. She reflects back on the first time that her husband went into a rage. He was throwing things all over the place. He broke many things that night. Edward didn't behave this way until he and Flora had been married for about a year. It was at that time that he made a complete change, sadly, it was a change for the worse. Before Flora even opens her eyes, she feels the stickiness all over her face and body. The only air conditioning they have is a small window unit that doesn't work very well, so they don't turn it on. Flora feels the pain on her face. She lightly touches her face. She gets up slowly, her body is sore all over. She takes a cool shower. Even the water hurts as it hits her body. She dries herself off carefully. Not wanting to wake up Edward, she sits quietly in the corner of the bedroom on a foot stool and looks into the broken mirror that Edward broke years ago. She begins to apply her makeup. Investing in full coverage makeup is crucial for Flora. With a damp sponge, she begins the sad task of covering up the bruises on her face. She holds back the tears trying not to think about last night. All she wants to do right now is go to church, the only place that makes her feel safe. She's relieved that she was able to leave the house without waking up her husband. Edward has a habit of mouthing off negative comments to Flora when he knows that she's going to church. This is usually because he's still drunk or badly hungover. Every Sunday when Flora is in church, tears roll down her face as she's overwhelmed in God's presence. After a long week at work, Friday is finally here. While most people are celebrating the last day of the workweek, Flora is in agony wondering what the next two days will be like for her. It's six thirty and although Edward gets off work at three o'clock, Flora still comes home to an empty house. Later that night she calls his cell phone several times before he actually answers. "Yeah!" Edward says, as he answers the phone. With caller id, he knows darn well who's calling. His rudeness towards Flora is always enhanced when other people are around. "Hey, babe, where are you?" asks Flora. "Ugh, yeah, I had to help a co-worker. She needed some help with her sprinkler system." says Edward. "She?" asked Flora in an unsettling tone. "Yeah, it's just a lady I work with. I'm not sure how long I'll be." he says as his eyes almost bulge out of his head while watching his coworker walking out of the house. "I gotta go." Says Edward, as he ends the call. He's in disbelief and just stares. Is this his lucky day or what? This woman walked into her backyard stark naked. He can't help but notice her beautiful large breasts. Not to mention, the rest of her body. She jumps in

93

her pool and starts swimming laps. Although this woman is in her sixties, his animal urges have just surfaced. She gets out of the pool and reaches for a towel that sits on a chair. She wraps it around her and sits down on a lawn chair. Edward is finishing up on repairing the leaky pipe in the backyard. He walks over towards her. "Okay, your pipe is fixed. You shouldn't have any more problems, but if you do, please call me. I will be more than happy to come back. "Sit," says the woman. "Okay." says Edward. "Wanna beer?' she asks. "Yeah, that sounds great," he says. She confidently walks over to her pool house and grabs a couple of beers from the refrigerator. The woman is talking to him for a while, as they drink they're beer. Edward is so excited at this point. "Excuse me for saying this, but your body is so perfect. I've never seen such beauty. "Oh, honey, thanks. I have an amazing plastic surgeon that has performed miracles on this body. I even had my va-jay-jay redone." she says, as she gets up to get more beer. "Wow, you look great, but what made you do this?" asked Edward, as he tries to play it cool, not wanting to reveal just how excited he really is. "My husband!" she responds. "He made you do it?" asked Edward. "No, no, it was all my idea. I thought if I could have the perfect body, my husband's penis would get hard again, but the plan failed. My days of having sex with my husband had been over since I was in my forties. I did all this work for nothing." she says. "Where is your husband?" asked Edward. "Dead! He died years ago." she responded. "Don't you have a boyfriend?' Edward asked in anticipation. "I do, but hell, his parts don't work either." she says as she stands up and takes her towel off. She jumps back in the pool. "You mind if I join you? asked Edward, while taking off his t-shirt. "Please, jump on in." she says, as she's in awe of Edwards tight abs and dark colored skin. He slowly unzipped his jeans. As he pulls them down, his fully aroused penis pops straight out of his pants. That's a view that she hasn't seen in many years. "Wow, that looks so delicious. It's been so long since I had a penis inside of me." She says, looking down at his crotch. She's instantly so horny just thinking about him entering her body. He swims towards her. Supporting her upper body, she places both arms on the concrete at the edge of the pool. She quickly spreads and raises her legs in the air as she giggles. Edward can't get to her fast enough. He enters her wet snatch instantly. Loving every moment of his hard cock pounding her repeatedly, she moans and yells in ecstasy. They have the most incredible sex for hours upon hours. Happy and completely satisfied, they both fall asleep on a blanket under the moon. Flora has been pacing the floors all night. She knows. She knows all too well that he's being unfaithful. Her gut is telling her that. This is not the first time, nor will it be the last. She's repeatedly forgiven his infidelities. It's morning and Flora is awakened by the noise of the front door opening. It's Edward, and he heads straight to the shower. Flora walks into the bathroom. "Where have you been?" she asked. "I went to the icehouse with the guys, and drank so much that I passed out in the car." he responds, while washing his hair. "Edward, I called you so many times last night. How come you never answered the phone?" asked Flora, not buying his story. "No, you didn't," he responds. "Were you with another woman?" asked Flora. "We'll talk when I get out of the shower. Just get out." he says, avoiding the question. He gets dressed and goes into the kitchen, where Flora is cooking the usual Sunday morning breakfast. "Why was the back door unlocked?" asked Edward in a mad tone. "What? The back door was not unlocked." responds Flora. "Who came over last night?" yells Edward as he slaps Flora across her face. "Nobody." responds Flora in a defensive way. "You're having an affair!" yells Edward as he slaps her again. "No, no, I would never." says Flora in a confused and nervous tone, not knowing where this was all coming from. "You're sleeping around, letting men come into our house at night. I want a divorce!" says Edward. "What? Why? No, Edward, I would never cheat on you. You have to believe me," cries Flora. Over the next few weeks, Edward lies to everyone, saying that he's getting a divorce because his wife is cheating on him. This is all to hide his master plan. His plan to move in with his lady co-worker that he's continued to bone every chance he gets. She's older, yes, but she's rich. In his eyes, he's hit the jackpot. Flora is devastated. She spends her days and nights crying. She's confused as to why Edward is behaving this way, but every time she confronts him, he starts hitting her. She's so embarrassed about the lies that he's spreading about her. She's applying so much makeup on her face, trying to hide all the bruises. She's never cheated, and Edward knows that. She meets up with her girlfriends and is getting drunk often, not knowing what to do. Soon, she becomes angry. She starts selling all of his belongings one by one. Since Edward only comes home at night, he doesn't notice that his things are missing. Once he reveals his plan to his lady lover, he's put in his place really quick. "You're not moving in with me. I have a boyfriend, and he wants to get married this year." she says, while shaking her head. "What do you mean? We have something pretty awesome going on here." Edward responds. "It's sex! That's all! Simply sex. I am not looking for a relationship with you. You're married and have kids. I don't want any part of that. Look, you can come over from time to time, but once I get married, that will be over." She responds. "Come on? Don't you want to be with someone who can satisfy you and make all your fantasies come true? That boyfriend of yours can't even get it up." Says Edward. "Oh, honey, grow up. It's been fun, but I can't be in a relationship with you. Besides, I'm in love with my boyfriend, and his millions. She sees how disappointed that Edward is. Honey, I have money, but I need someone with more money than me. I love my lifestyle and I don't want to change any of it. You would never be able to provide the life that I'm used to." She says,

Weeks go by and there is no changing her mind.

Edward tells his wife that he forgives her and is willing to work out the marriage. Flora knows that he knows she never did anything wrong. He pulls off this scheme every time he starts sleeping around with someone new. She's gotten used to Edwards lies, alcoholism, and abuse. As always, she doesn't take any action and continues to live an exhausting life behind the makeup.

Seeking her Husband's Love

It's a nice day at Garner State Park, people come from different parts of the world to enjoy it.

"Can you take a picture of me?" Sandra asks her husband, Jose. "Ugh. Why? responds Jose in a rude tone. Sandra instantly feels bad when Jose talks to her like that. She often feels like such a nuisance to him. "You already have the camera out." replies Sandra. "Yeah, but I'm taking pictures of the scenery." Says Jose as he walks off in another direction. Sandra walks quickly after him. "Well, why not take a picture of me in front of the scenery?" Asks Sandra, which is now out of breath, trying to catch up to him. Jose stops and turns around. "Really?" He says in a mad tone. That look of hate in his eyes is something that Sandra sees often. "Forget it." Responds Sandra, as she sadly walks away. Jose doesn't pay any mind to Sandra. He walks ahead and looks around at everything with great enthusiasm. Sandra is saddened, once again. Jose is ignoring her. He's always been the silent and mysterious type. This macho trait is what Sandra found intriguing when she first met Jose. She never would have thought that his silence would change to rudeness towards her. Later that evening, they were having dinner. Jose has a way of controlling the room, simply by his silence. He was not a talker, and he didn't like others to talk either. The sound of others talking simply annoyed Jose. "Babe, why don't you like taking pictures of me? Asked Sandra in a shaky voice. She was always nervous to speak, because most of the time, he would respond with anger. "Are you serious?" Is all Jose said.

"Gosh, Babe, why can't you just be happy when you're with me. If you truly love me, you would enjoy taking pictures of me. She says. "You're always getting mad at stupid shit." He says, "Stupid shit? All I wanted was for you to take a picture of me at the park with that beautiful background. What is so wrong with that? Why did you have to get so angry and walk off? Many times, I feel like you don't even love me at all." Cries Sandra with tears rolling down her face. "Look!" Shouts Jose as he stands up. "I go to work! I pay the bills! What more do you want?" He shouts as he storms out of the kitchen. Sandra gets up and attempts to run after him. He slams the bedroom door and locks it. She tries to open the door. "Jose, please, unlock the door." She falls down to her knees. "I just want you to love me, Jose. That's all I want. I don't want to feel like I'm a nuisance to you. I want to be your special girl. Cries Sandra. Jose never says a word. The night goes by and he doesn't come out of the room. He goes to sleep without any remorse. Sandra finally falls asleep on the couch. The next morning, Sandra is awakened by the sound of loud banging. She throws off the couch pillows that she had covered herself with during the night when she got cold. She gets up and walks slowly, following the sound that is leading her to the kitchen. She sees Jose. He's unloading the dishwasher. He's just about throwing the dishes in the cabinet, and slamming the cabinet doors. "What's going on?" Asked Sandra. Jose doesn't say a word. He continues to toss the silverware in the drawer. "You okay?" she asked in a trembling voice, wishing she was wearing a suit of armor, afraid that she's about to be attacked by the unleashing of her husband's rage. Jose doesn't respond. She goes to the restroom to brush her teeth and wash her face. She stares into the mirror. She sees a sad soul looking back at her. She hears Jose leaving the house. She then begins to get ready for work. She works the front desk of a local museum of antiques, where many tourists come through. She arrives and puts on her happy face. Later that afternoon, a young man walks in. "Pardon me?" He says.

"Yes, how can I help you?" Responds Sandra with a smile. "May I please take a picture of you in front of the antique wooden wagon?" He asked. "Oh, ugh, how about if I take a picture of you standing in front of it instead?" Asked Sandra. "Oh no, not of me. I hope I'm not being too forward, but you're much prettier than me. This will make the perfect picture to hang in my shop. You know, a beautiful girl, in front of a nice antique wagon. Now, that will make a nice wall picture for my grand opening. Says the gentleman. You're welcome to pop in anytime you'd like. It's just up the road from here. As a matter of fact, the ribbon cutting will be next month. He says, Sandra smiles. "Okay, I will be honored to be in your picture. She says, as she walks towards the wagon. She smiles and he takes the photo. "Ma'am, thank you so much. This truly means so much to me." He says, as he walks away with a big smile. Several weeks later, Jose is opening up his Sunday paper and lays it out on the kitchen table, as he always does. His eyes are locked in on the picture that has made the front page. He blinks his eyes, trying to focus. Maybe he's seeing things. He thinks. "Is that? Is that my wife?" He asked himself. "Sandra! Sandra! Get your ass in here!" He yells. Sandra was putting away some clean laundry when she heard him. She rushes over to the kitchen. "What's wrong? She responds. "What the hell is this? He shouts as he waves the newspaper in the air, then slams it down on the table. She looks at the paper. Her eyes get bigger and bigger, as she can clearly see that it's the photo that the gentleman took of her in front of the wagon at her job. The handsome owner is standing tall and proud in front of picture. Proud of not only the grand opening of his new shop, but you can see he's proud to be standing in front of this oversized wall picture. Sandra can't help but smile. A picture of her is not only in this man's shop, but it has made the front page of their city's newspaper. "Wow. that's me." She says, in a low voice. She can't wipe the smile off her face. "Oh, you think that's funny." He says, "Who took this picture? And, why the hell are you in this picture?

Who is this guy? Are you cheating on me? Say something?" Yells Jose. "No, I'm not cheating on you. This nice man came into the museum and asked if he could take a picture of me in front of the old wagon. I didn't want to at first, but he explained he wanted this as an entry photo for his new shop. It made me happy that somebody wanted to take a picture of me, so I did." She responds, feeling quite good about herself. She stands a little taller and walks back to the bedroom to finish her laundry. Jose crumbles the newspaper and throws it across the room. "You mean to tell me that a picture of you is going to be in this man's shop? He yells as he follows her. "Yes, it is. She responds. "I can't believe you agreed to that." shouts Jose. "Why are you so mad?" She asked. "You don't even like taking pictures of me. I've asked you so many times to take a picture of me. You never do. This nice person was actually excited to take a picture of me. So, I let him." She says, "Doesn't it make you proud to have your wife's picture at a local business? She asked. "I'm humiliated! I hope nobody I know will ever see it." He says, as he rushes out of the house. He gets in his truck and burns rubber as he peels out of the driveway, causing a scene. Sandra looks out the window as she watches him leave. She knows that if she stays married to Jose, she will spend her life seeking her husband's love.

Take that Leap

Many women stay married to men who cheat and abuse them repeatedly.

This is an exhausting lifestyle. If this type of life doesn't kill these women, it will certainly age them quickly.

The stress is written all over their face and many people see it clearly.

Some women don't feel worthy.

Women, you must learn to respect yourselves and never expect anything less from others.

Don't ever give anyone power over you. Learn to love yourself so much that you could never tolerate anyone to treat you badly.

Find your strength and say "NO" to a man who wants to control or disrespect you.

There are also women out there that are too scared to leave these abusive relationships for fear of their life or the safety of their children, or they don't have money or a job.

Let me point out that there is an enormous amount of help out there.

The National Domestic Hotline has helped millions in making that step. You can call them anytime at 1-800-799-7233

There comes a time that you **should** walk away.

A few women out there are simply not motivated to make changes in their life.

They're comfortable and they've accepted this way of life.

Maybe they have small children and don't want to break up the family.

Children are resilient. Most will adapt just fine.

We all know that children are smart and know exactly what's going on.

The longer they see their mother being abused and cheated on, the more likely they will repeat that cycle.

In our society, it's common for men to cheat and it's not a big deal to anyone. Many men are proud of cheating and share this with friends. The more women they cheat with, the bigger their ego.

On the flipside, if a woman cheats, she's trash and the whole town will be talking about her. That's just how it is. There's nothing that anyone can ever do about that.

A husband is unlikely to forgive a cheating wife. Men are too proud and macho to stay married to a woman who has betrayed him.

An unhappy wife can be at the cliff for a very long time, not knowing when to take that leap.

Each time her husband cheats and abuses her, she gets closer and closer to the edge of the cliff.

One day, she may take that leap.

A leap of faith, a leap to be free, a leap to finally be happy.

THE END

www.ingramcontent.com/pod-product-compliance
Lightning Source LLC
Chambersburg PA
CBHW06075318062 6
46818CB00002B/558